BLACKSMITH'S SONG

A new generation begins: for Will, Declan, Fionnula, Ainsley, and Eliza
—E. A. V.

Thank you President Obama, and Governor Cuomo, for the ACA and the
NY State of Health Exchange, which saved my life and allowed me to finish this book.
—A. R.

Published by
PEACHTREE PUBLISHING COMPANY INC.
1700 Chattahoochee Avenue
Atlanta, Georgia 30318-2112
PeachtreeBooks.com

Text © 2018 by Elizabeth Van Steenwyk
Illustrations © 2018 by Anna Rich

First trade paperback edition published in 2022

Edited by Kathy Landwehr
Art direction by Nicola Simmonds Carmack

The paintings were created in oils.

Printed and bound in August 2022 at Leo Paper, Heshan, China.
10 9 8 7 6 5 4 3 2 1 (hardcover)
10 9 8 7 6 5 4 3 2 1 (trade paperback)
HC ISBN: 978-1-56145-580-5
PB ISBN: 978-1-68263-480-6

Library of Congress Cataloging-in-Publication Data

Van Steenwyk, Elizabeth.
Blacksmith's song / written by Elizabeth Van Steenwyk ; illustrated by Anna Rich.
pages cm
Summary: "The son of a blacksmith and slave learns that his father is using the rhythm of his hammering
to communicate with travelers on the Underground Railroad"—Provided by publisher.
ISBN: 978-1-56145-580-5
1. Underground Railroad—Juvenile fiction. [1. Underground Railroad—Fiction. 2. Fugitive slaves—Fiction.
3. Slavery—Fiction.] I. Rich, Anna, 1956- illustrator. II. Title.
PZ7.V358Bl 2013
[E]—dc23 2012033079
20 12033079

BLACKSMITH'S SONG

Written by Elizabeth Van Steenwyk
Illustrated by Anna Rich

Ω
PEACHTREE
ATLANTA

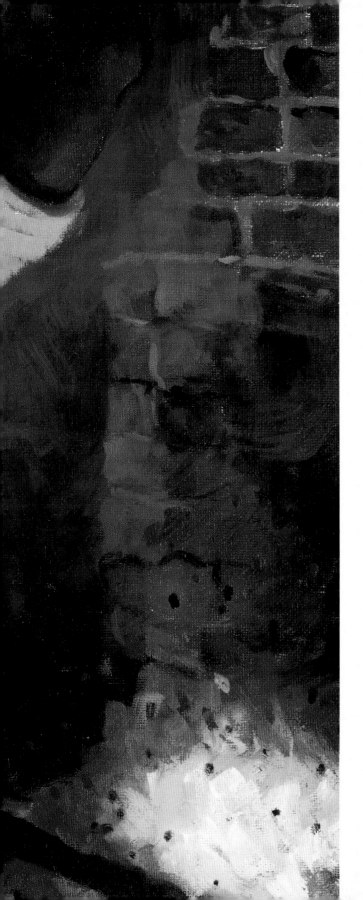

Pa is tired and feverish looking, but he's already up and blowing on the fire when I get up.

"Let me help, Pa," I say.

He doesn't answer and my words drift away like smoke.

His muscles glisten. He's working hard, but the sound from his anvil has no rhythm this afternoon. It's an ordinary song for an ordinary day.

Some evenings, Pa pounds out the blacksmith's song, a deep-down rhythm of hammer striking anvil. The sound grows louder, faster, as his tap, tap, tapping tells listening ears and hearts that the waiting is nearly over.

Tonight he is sending word to the folks in the woods, who are waiting to hear when it's time to leave.

"Ma," I ask. "When will it be our turn?"

"Soon," she whispers. "You be ready when Pa plays for us."

"I'm ready now," I tell her. I'm only nine, but the song of leaving is in my heart too.

That night, sounds scratch at my dreams, trying to get in.

Are the people out there afraid in the darkness?

Will I be brave when it's our turn to go?

The next day, we go about our business. Though he is weak, Pa makes horseshoes and wagon wheels. Ma cooks and serves, and I take care of the chickens.

"Give me all your eggs," I tell the hens, "so Ma can make lots of cakes for the missus."

The hens don't care about cakes. They just care about me taking away what's theirs. Same as us.

I practice tapping Pa's rhythms on the henhouse, but it worries the chickens, so I quit.

About noontime, some white people
drive up to the master's house in their fine
carriages.

Later, Ma tells us what she heard while
she was serving dinner. Those white people
were looking for their slaves who ran away
in the night.

Has anyone heard after them? they ask.

No, says the master.

Good thing they don't ask Ma.

"Tell me again how you learned the traveling rhythm," I ask Pa the next morning. I like to hear the story again and again.

Sparks fly from his hammer. "Learned it from my pa," he says. "Just like he learned it from his. Grandpa noticed the rhythms first and put some meaning to them. Soon, the understanding of it spread to others. Now lots of folks use those same rhythms to tell about the freedom trail."

"Let me try," I beg. "I'm ready now."

Pa puts down his hammer and wipes his sweaty face with a rag. He looks frail. "Soon," he says.

I pick up his hammer and strike the anvil.

"Not now," he whispers. "Later."

The master comes in. Has he heard us?

"Are you done with the present for the missus?" he asks Pa. "It's almost time for her birthday party."

"I'm working on it now," Pa says.

A bird slowly emerges from a piece of hot iron as Pa shapes its birth with a hammer and tong.

"This will sit atop the garden gate," he tells the master.

As the sun sets, word seeps down to us. More folks are coming along the freedom trail. It's almost time for a song from the blacksmith.

Will this be our time to leave as well?

Pa's rhythms begin. Tapping softly, tap, tap, tapping.

I stomp my feet to the rhythm.

I clap my hands.

I can pound this rhythm out just like Pa does. Hammer strikes anvil. I sway to the rhythms and listen.

The moon is a stingy slice and dark surrounds our cabin. I hear whispers, and footsteps, and dogs. And then there's the steady clop of horses' hooves and white men's voices.

I hold my breath until I'm ready to burst.

Pa comes in late, when it's quiet again. Sleeping is sparse in our cabin. Our ears don't quit listening until dawn.

After I've tended the chickens the next morning, I go to help Pa. The fever has gripped him bad, but he's hard at work at his anvil.

Midmorning, the master pays another call. "Why were you at your forge so late last night?" he asks Pa.

"I was finishing the garden gate for the missus's birthday," Pa says.

On the day of the party, Pa and I place the new gate at the entrance to the rose garden. He is so weak that I have to help him.

The fancy folks marvel at Pa's artistry. Music plays and people laugh and talk.

I sense an unfelt rhythm, an unheard song. Surely it will be soon for us.

But how will Pa pound out the news to everybody else when he's feeling so poorly?

In bed, I hear the noise of the party, but not the sound I've been waiting for. Pa lies on his pallet, weak and feverish and unable to send out the traveling rhythm.

My eyes won't close. I tap out a message on my hand, just for me.

Ma arrives late. "Quickly," she whispers to Pa. "It's time." He tries to get up, but he doesn't have the strength. She looks at him, and then at me. We both know.

"I have to do it," I tell her. "I have to be the one to send the news."

I try not to think about the dark and the danger waiting outside. And maybe the dogs.

I pick up a hammer in the blacksmith's shed. I choose the smallest one; I know my size.

I can still hear the music and laughter from the party.

But another rhythm beats in my heart and soul, just like it does in Pa's and did in his pa's before that. I strike the anvil and send the message to those waiting in the woods, who are hoping to hear the blacksmith's song.

At last, it is our turn too. We wait to leave until the party is loudest. Ma and I have to help Pa up the hill. Then we hurry to the woods.

Just before we step into the thicket of trees, the three of us turn to look at the blacksmith's shed one last time. In the darkness, the forge still glows with the heat of Pa's last song—and my first.

Pa's anvil is silent now, but maybe
soon its message will be heard again,
when another blacksmith picks up
a hammer and sends others on their
journey.

He presses something into my hand.
It's an iron star.

"To light our way to freedom," he
whispers.

Author's Note

Blacksmith's Song is fiction, but it is inspired by stories about communication along the Underground Railroad.

Neither a railroad nor underground, the Underground Railroad was a secret (thus "underground") network of trails, meeting points, and safe houses that enslaved people used to escape, mostly to the North and Canada. There, they could live as free men and women. Along the way, they were aided by their fellow enslaved people, free-born Black people, Native Americans, and white abolitionists. Railroad terminology was used to refer to aspects of the journey—escapees were called travelers; those who guided them, conductors; and stopping places, stations.

The Underground Railroad was most active beginning around 1830 and throughout the Civil War (1861–1865). Somewhere between twenty-five thousand and one hundred thousand people may have escaped using this route, out of more than four million enslaved.

Aiding escaped enslaved people was illegal, even in the North. Violating the Fugitive Slave Act of 1850 could result in punishment of six months in prison and a thousand-dollar fine. An enslaved person who was caught trying to escape or aid in another's escape would be brutally punished and often sold.

Enslaved people were, of course, prohibited from talking to each other about methods and routes for escape. Doing so would have been incredibly dangerous. There are many theories about how they might have communicated with each other about the Underground Railroad, but little evidence to support these beliefs. Some methods described in folklore are visual—such as quilts and dance—and others are oral—like code words, songs, and perhaps the rhythm of the blacksmith's hammer.